This book belongs to

There was an old lady who swallowed a fly

Kate Toms

make
believe
ideas

There was an **old lady** who **swallowed** a fly. **Why**, oh **why**, did she swallow a **fly?**

Oh my, oh my!

Tra la la!

That little old lady
was **walking** along,

enjoying the sunshine

and **singing** a song.

When **all of a sudden**

a fly flew **south** . . .

and ended up flying

right into her **mouth!**

That poor old lady – what a to-do!

Imagine if that happened

to **you!**

The fly now buzzes and tickles her tummy
(she didn't think it tasted so yummy)!

But suddenly she has an idea
to make the naughty fly disappear:

to catch the fly she swallows a spider –

so now she has them both inside her!

Oh my, oh my!

Down by the pond
she **spots** a **frog**,
sitting still on a **speckled** log.

Without even saying
"How do you do?"

she picks up the frog and
swallows
him too!

cRoAK!

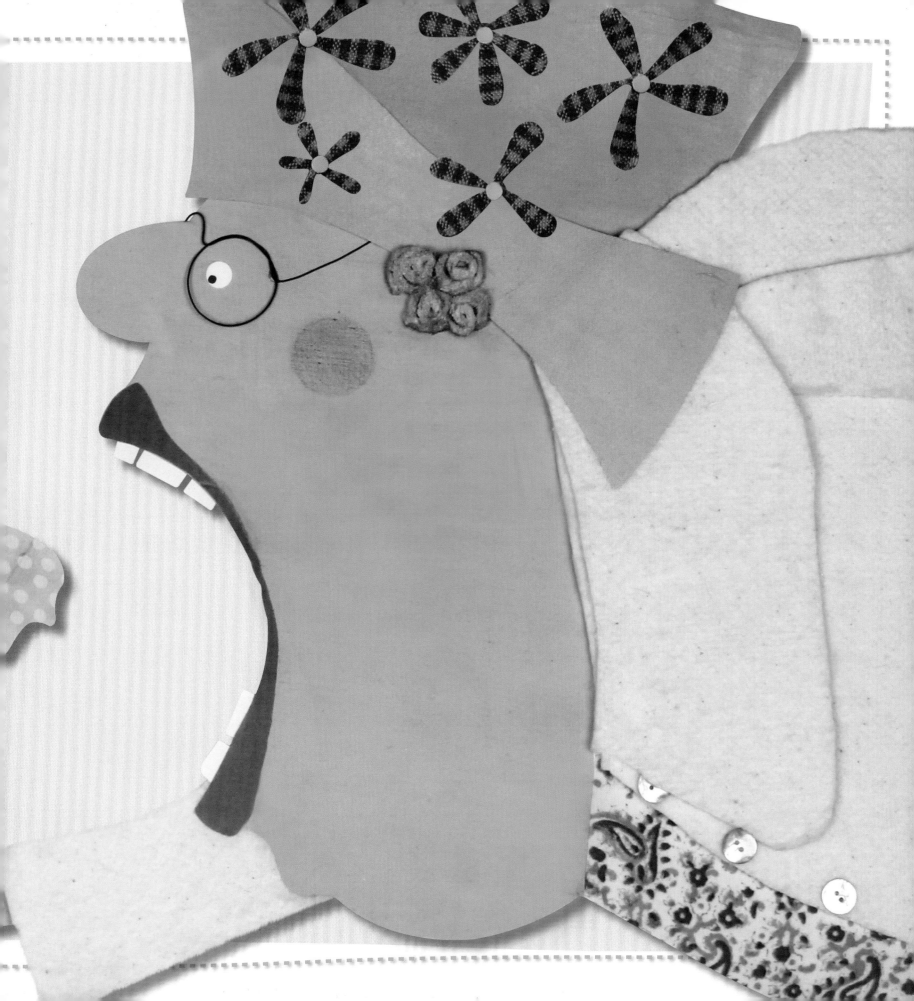

Feeling just a **little queasy**
(certainly not so bright and breezy),
she **spots** a heron on a nest –

I wonder if **you** can **guess** the rest?

How **absurd** . . .

to swallow a **bird!**

Oh my, oh my!

How could she **do** that?
We **don't** know how –
but you won't **believe**
what happens now . . .

Pretty Kitty
sits and **purrs;**
from **behind** her something **stirs.**

Before **poor puss**
has time
to flee . . .

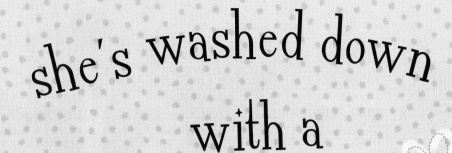

she's washed down
with a
cup of
tea!

Fancy **that,**
to swallow a **cat!**

Oh my, oh my!

By this time it's **getting dark**. Prince the **dog** plays in the park.

But poor old Prince
just does not see
the **old lady**
lurking by a big tree.

GULP!

Poor Prince . . .

The old lady's
tummy is
fit to **burst** –
she wished
she'd thought more
carefully first.

She swallowed the **dog**

to catch the cat.

She swallowed the **cat**

to catch the bird.

She swallowed the **bird**

to catch the frog.

She swallowed the **frog**

to catch the spider.

She swallowed the **spider**

to catch the fly . . .

if **only** that fly had just **flown by.**

Oh my, oh my!